Disney · PIXAR

TOY STORY 2

Adapted by Diane Muldrow

Illustrated by the Disney Creative Development Storybook Art Staff

A Random House PICTUREBACK® Book

Random House 🏠 New York

Copyright © 1999, 2003 Disney Enterprises, Inc./Pixar Animation Studios. Original *Toy Story* elements © Disney Enterprises, Inc. All rights reserved under International and Pan-American Copyright Conventions. Published in the United States by Random House Children's Books, a division of Random House, Inc., New York, and simultaneously in Canada by Random House of Canada Limited, Toronto, in conjunction with Disney Enterprises, Inc. Originally published in slightly different form by Golden Books in 1999. PICTUREBACK, RANDOM HOUSE, and the Random House colophon are registered trademarks of Random House, Inc. Mr. Potato Head® is a registered trademark of Hasbro, Inc. Used with permission. © Hasbro, Inc. All rights reserved. Slinky® Dog © James Industries. Library of Congress Control Number: 2002107818   ISBN: 0-7364-2129-7 www.randomhouse.com/kids/disney
Printed in the United States of America   10 9 8 7 6 5 4 3 2 1
First Random House Edition 2003

"It's Cowboy Camp time!" shouted Andy. He picked up Woody, his favorite toy cowboy. Woody loved Cowboy Camp. It was that special weekend every summer when he and Andy went away together.

Before leaving, Andy played a game with Woody and Buzz Lightyear. But the game got too rough, and Woody's arm went *r-r-rip!*

There was no time to fix Woody's arm before Andy left. So he decided to leave Woody at home.

Woody couldn't believe it! He watched sadly as Andy went off to camp . . . without him.

A few hours later, Andy's mom began setting out tables and boxes for a yard sale. Before Woody realized what was happening, Wheezy—a toy penguin who had lost his squeak— was taken outside to be sold.

With the help of Andy's puppy, Buster, Woody rode to the rescue, determined to save the squeakless penguin!

Buster made it safely back inside with Wheezy, but Woody had fallen off the puppy and was lying on the ground.

A man at the yard sale picked him up. "I can't believe it!" the man said. "I found him! I found him! I'll give you fifty dollars for this," he said to Andy's mom.

"Sorry, he's not for sale," said Andy's mom. But when she wasn't
looking, the man put Woody into the trunk of his car and drove off.
Buzz Lightyear saw what was happening from Andy's room
upstairs. He raced out the window to try to save Woody, but he was
too late. The last thing Buzz saw was the toynapper's license plate.

Woody soon found himself in a strange new place. The toynapper set him down and left.

Woody saw that he was face to face with three strange toys—an old prospector, a cowgirl, and a horse.

"It's you! It's you!" cried the cowgirl. She was really happy to see Woody.

"We've waited countless years for this day!" said the Prospector. Woody looked confused. He didn't know what they meant.

"You don't know who you are, do you?" the Prospector asked.

Woody noticed an old magazine with his picture on the cover. And an old TV played *Woody's Roundup*, a program from 1950 featuring the world's favorite cowboy, Sheriff Woody. His sidekicks were Jessie, the yodeling cowgirl; Stinky Pete, the Prospector; and Bullseye, the sharpest horse in the West.

Woody couldn't believe his eyes and ears. He was famous!

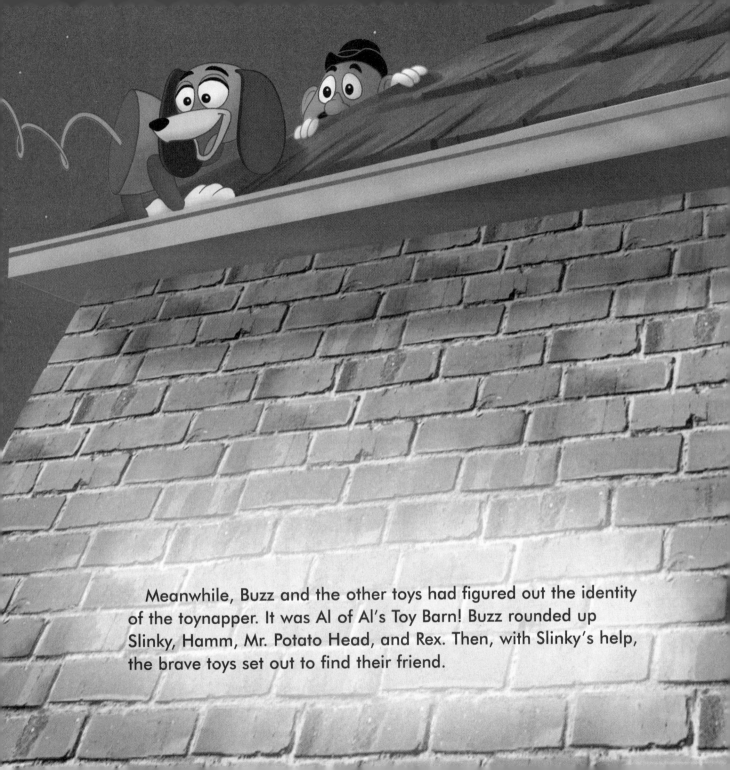

Meanwhile, Buzz and the other toys had figured out the identity of the toynapper. It was Al of Al's Toy Barn! Buzz rounded up Slinky, Hamm, Mr. Potato Head, and Rex. Then, with Slinky's help, the brave toys set out to find their friend.

Back at Al's apartment, Woody was having fun playing with his new friends. "Now it's on to the museum! We're being sold to the Konishi Toy Museum in Japan," said the Prospector.

"Japan? I can't go to Japan," said Woody. "I've got to get back to Andy."

Soon Woody's arm was repaired and he was ready to go home.

But then Jessie told Woody her story. She had once belonged to a little girl, but when the girl grew up, she gave Jessie away.

"Could Andy outgrow me one day?" Woody wondered. He decided to stay with the *Woody's Roundup* gang after all.

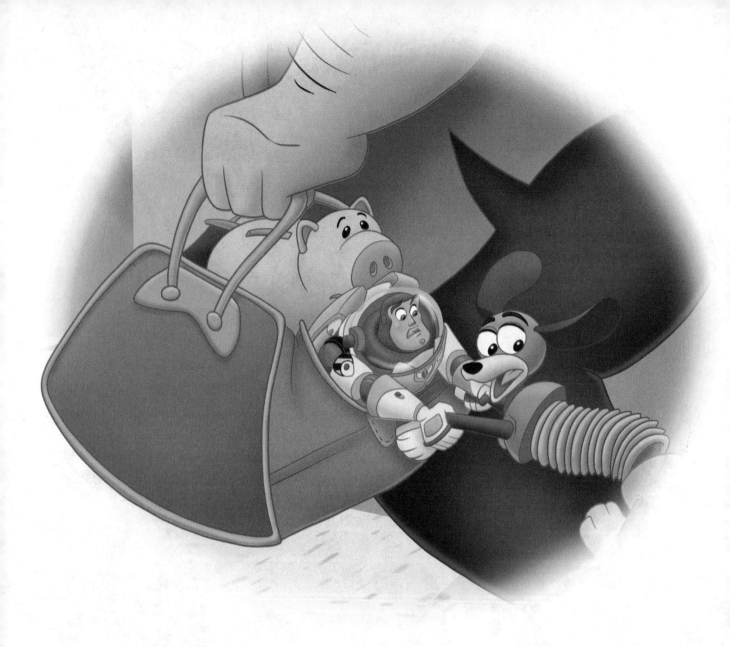

Just then, Buzz and the others reached the end of their long
journey—they were inside Al's Toy Barn.
The toys found Al's office and snuck into his bag.

Soon the toys found themselves in Al's apartment.
"We're here to rescue you," Buzz told Woody.
But Woody didn't want to be rescued. "Andy is growing up,
and one day he won't need me any longer," said Woody. "I can't
abandon these guys. They need me to get into the museum.
Without me, they'll go back into storage . . . maybe forever."

"YOU ARE A TOY!" Buzz shouted. But when he saw the look on Woody's face, he gave up. "Let's go, everyone," he said sadly.

As Andy's toys turned to leave, Woody caught sight of something on television. The Woody on TV was singing to a little boy. Suddenly Woody realized his mistake. He knew he belonged with Andy. Quickly he ran to escape through the vent. But the Prospector blocked his way!

"You are not going!" said the Prospector. "I've waited too long for this, and you are not ruining my plans."

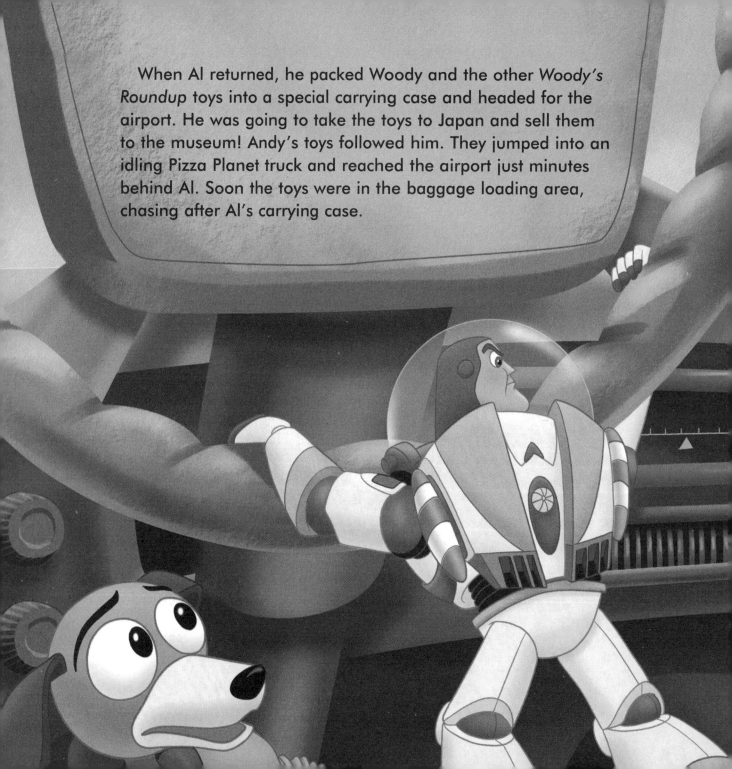

When Al returned, he packed Woody and the other *Woody's Roundup* toys into a special carrying case and headed for the airport. He was going to take the toys to Japan and sell them to the museum! Andy's toys followed him. They jumped into an idling Pizza Planet truck and reached the airport just minutes behind Al. Soon the toys were in the baggage loading area, chasing after Al's carrying case.

Buzz found Al's case moving along on a conveyor belt.
The Prospector leaped out and started to fight Buzz. Working
together, Woody and Buzz managed to stuff the Prospector into
a child's backpack.

Meanwhile, Jessie was still in the case, headed for the airplane! Woody chased the carrying case onto the plane and got her out. But when he opened the escape hatch, the plane's wheels started moving. They were trapped!

Using his pull string as a lasso, Woody swung down with Jessie just as Buzz and Bullseye galloped up to them. Woody and Jessie landed safely on Bullseye's back.

Together, the toys made it home just before Andy returned from Cowboy Camp. Andy was thrilled with Jessie and Bullseye and started making up games for them.

After his great adventure, Woody sure was glad to be back in Andy's room. As for Jessie and Bullseye, they were thrilled to be part of a family again.